MORE SPECIAL OFFERS
FOR MR MEN AND LITTLE MISS READERS

50p

In every Mr Men and Little Miss book lik[...]
sticker and activity books, you will find a sp[...]e
will send you a gift [...]
Choose either a <u>Mr Men</u> or <u>Little Miss</u> [...]
double sided full colour bedroo[...]

D0537500

Return this page **with six tokens per gift required** to:
Marketing Dept., MM / LM, World International Ltd.,
PO Box 7, Manchester, M19 2HD

Your name:_____ Age: _____

Address: _____

_____

_____Postcode: _____

Parent / Guardian Name (Please Print)_____

Please tape a 20p coin to your request to cover part post and package cost

I enclose <u>six</u> tokens per gift, and 20p please send me:-

Posters:-

Door Hangers -

Mr Men Poster		Little Miss Poster	☐
Mr Nosey / Muddle		Mr Greedy / Lazy	☐
Mr Tickle / Grumpy		Mr Slow / Busy	☐
Mr Messy / Quiet		Mr Perfect / Forgetful	☐
L Miss Fun / Late		L Miss Helpful / Tidy	☐
L Miss Busy / Brainy		L Miss Star / Fun	☐

20p

Stick 20p here please

Please Tick Appropriate Box

Collect six of these tokens
You will find one inside every
Mr Men and Little Miss book
which has this special offer.

1 TOKEN

We may occasionally wish to advise you of other Mr Men gifts.
If you would rather we didn't please tick this box ☐

Offer open to residents of UK, Channel Isles and Ireland only

Mr Men and Little Miss Library Presentation Boxes

In response to the many thousands of requests for the above, we are delighted to advise that these are now available direct from ourselves,
for only **£4.99** (inc VAT) plus 50p p&p.
The full colour boxes accommodate each complete library. They have an integral carrying handle as well as a neat stay closed fastener.
Please do not send cash in the post. Cheques should be made payable to **World International Ltd. for the sum of £5.49** (inc p&p) per box.

Please note books are not included.

Please return this page with your cheque, stating below which presentation box you would like, to:-
Mr Men Office, World International
PO Box 7, Manchester, M19 2HD

Your name:_____

Address: _____

_____

_____Postcode: _____

Name of Parent/Guardian (please print):_____

Signature:_____

I enclose a cheque for £_____ made payable to World International Ltd.,

Please send me a Mr Men Presentation Box ☐

        Little Miss Presentation Box ☐   (please tick or write in quantity) and allow 28 days for delivery

Thank you

Offer applies to UK, Eire & Channel Isles only

MR.GRUMBLE

MR. GRUMBLE

by Roger Hargreaves

WORLD INTERNATIONAL

Mr Grumble's name suited him well!

"Bah!" he would grumble, every morning,
when his alarm clock rang.
"It's the start of yet another
horrible day!"

"Bah!" he would groan every afternoon,
on his walk in the country.
"I hate the countryside!"

One day, just after he had said this,
someone suddenly appeared by magic.

It was a wizard.

A wizard, to whom Mr Grumble had the
nerve to say, "Bah! I hate wizards who
suddenly appear by magic."

"Really?" said the wizard.
"Well, I don't like people who are constantly
grumbling and moaning. I'll tell you what
I do to people who have bad manners.
I turn them into …

… little pigs!"

And the wizard disappeared,
leaving behind him a very piggy
looking Mr Grumble.

Mr Grumble was afraid that he might
remain a pig for the rest of his life.

But five minutes later,
by magic, of course,
he changed back into his old self.

He set off again and happened to pass
Little Miss Fun's house.

"Come in!" she cried.
"I'm having a party!"

Mr Grumble went in, but when he heard
Little Miss Fun's guests singing and
laughing he scowled.

"Bah!" he moaned.
"I can't stand singing and laughing!"

He would have done better to
have kept quiet, because …

… the wizard appeared once more.

"I see that my first lesson
wasn't enough!" he said.
"If I'm going to teach you to stop grumbling,
groaning and moaning, I'll have to do
more than turn you into a little pig,
I'll have to turn you into …

… a big pig!"

Mr Grumble did not like it one bit.

Little Miss Fun and her guests, however,
found it very funny.

"Please," begged Mr Grumble,
"turn me back to normal!
I promise that I will never grumble,
groan or moan ever again!"

And he feebly wiggled his curly tail.

The wizard took pity on him,
and changed him back into his old self.

And then the wizard disappeared again.

Then Little Miss Fun jumped on to a table
and pretended to be a clown.

Mr Grumble was not amused.

"Bah!" he snorted.
"I can't stand people who jump on to tables
and pretend to be clowns!"

You can guess what happened next.

He turned into …

… an enormous pig!

An enormous pig whose face was
red with embarrassment!

"Oink!" wailed Mr Grumble, mournfully.

Then, this enormous red-faced pig,
made a solemn promise.

"Never again will I grumble, groan,
moan or snort!"

"Good," said the wizard,
suddenly appearing once again.

And Mr Grumble changed back
into his old self.

Well, not exactly his old self!

Look at that nice smile on his face.

Amazing, isn't it?

Later, Mr Grumble went home.

And, tired out after his exhausting day,
he went straight to bed.

He slept the whole night
without once grumbling,
groaning, moaning or snorting.

But not without …

… snoring!